This book belongs to

....

IMAGINE THAT™

Licensed exclusively to Imagine That Publishing Ltd
Tide Mill Way, Woodbridge, Suffolk, IP12 1AP, UK
www.imaginethat.com
Copyright © 2023 Imagine That Group Ltd
All rights reserved
0 2 4 6 8 9 7 5 3 1
Manufactured in Guangdong, China

ISBN 978-1-80105-630-4

5-minute
Dinosaur Stories

Contents

One Little Dinosaur

Written by **Pip Williams**

Illustrated by **Richard Watson**

The Loudest Roar!

Written by **Bodhi Hunter**

Illustrated by **Julia Seal**

Donut Touch!

Written by **Seb Davey**

Illustrated by **Alex Willmore**

We're Going on a Dino Hunt!
Written by **Yasmin Bond**

Illustrated by **Vicky Lommatzsch**

The Dinosaur Next Door
Written by **Bobbie Brooks**

Illustrated by **Rhys Waters**

Valley of the Dinosaurs
Written by **Oakley Graham**

Illustrated by **Ben Mantle**

One Little Dinosaur

Written by
Pip Williams

Illustrated by
Richard Watson

One little dinosaur counts
ten dotty rocks.

Two smart dinosaurs wear nine snazzy socks.

Three hungry dinosaurs eat eight yummy cakes.

Five curious dinosaurs follow six leaping frogs.

Six happy dinosaurs play with five noisy dogs.

Seven brave dinosaurs climb four rocky trails.

Eight stripy dinosaurs with three spots on their tails.

Nine dinosaurs roar and two dinosaurs wave.

Ten snoring dinosaurs
sleep in one big cave.

Dinosaurs can count
from one to ten...

And count from
ten to one again!

The Loudest Roar!

Written by
Bodhi Hunter

Illustrated by
Julia Seal

The forest was full of noisy dinosaurs, but Little Tyrannosaurus (tye-RAN-uh-SAWR-us) was sure that he could make the loudest noise of all.

"I'm going to prove it!" he told Papa Rex one day, and he set off to do just that, practicing his best roars as he went.

Soon, Little Tyrannosaurus found Triceratops (try-SAIR-uh-tops) who was grazing on some grass.

"Hello," said Little Tyrannosaurus. "Can you make a noise as loud as me?"

Triceratops let out the biggest noise that he could manage.
"BELLOW!"

Then Little Tyrannosaurus took a deep breath.
"ROOAARR!"
"Wow!" said Triceratops. "That is a loud roar!"

Next, Little Tyrannosaurus found
Ankylosaurus (ang-KILE-uh-SAWR-us).

"Can you make a noise as loud as me?" he asked.

Ankylosaurus swished her clubbed tail as hard as
she could against a tree. **"BOOM!"** went the tail.

Unimpressed, Little Tyrannosaurus roared so loudly the trees shook.

"ROOAARR!"

Ankylosaurus shook her head, "I could never make that much noise," she said.

Later that day, Little Tyrannosaurus spotted Diplodocus (dih-PLOD-uh-kus), munching on leaves from the tallest tree in the forest.

"Diplodocus, can you make a noise
as loud as me?" he shouted up.
"STOMP!"
went Diplodocus with his feet.

Then it was Little Tyrannosaurus' turn.

"ROOAARR!"

he roared at the top of his voice.

Diplodocus almost jumped out of his skin!

"I think you win!" Diplodocus laughed between eating mouthfuls of leaves.

Next, Little Tyrannosaurus met the raptors,
who were hunting for their dinner.

"Raptors, can you make a noise as loud as me?" he asked.

The raptors stopped what they were doing
and screeched with all of their might.
"SCREECH-SCREECH!"

It was a VERY loud noise, but Little Tyrannosaurus
let out his loudest roar so far.

"ROOAARR!"

"We can't beat that!" said the raptors.
"And you've scared away our dinner!"

Little Tyrannosaurus was very happy.
No other dinosaur in the whole forest
could make a sound as loud as him!

Then he heard a VERY big noise!
It was the loudest noise that Little
Tyrannosaurus had ever heard.

"ROOAARR!"

But where and who was
it coming from?

Little Tyrannosaurus was scared!
The VERY big noise got closer,
and closer, and closer, until finally...

"ROAR!"

Papa Rex appeared through the trees!

"I thought I was the loudest dinosaur in the forest!"
cried Little Tyrannosaurus, "but it's YOU, Papa! You're roarsome!"

"ROAR!"

"ROAR!"

"ROAR!"

Donut Touch!

Written by
Seb Davey

Illustrated by
Alex Willmore

This is Mikey...

These donuts are **mine!**
Keep your fingers away from them...

DO NOT TOUCH!

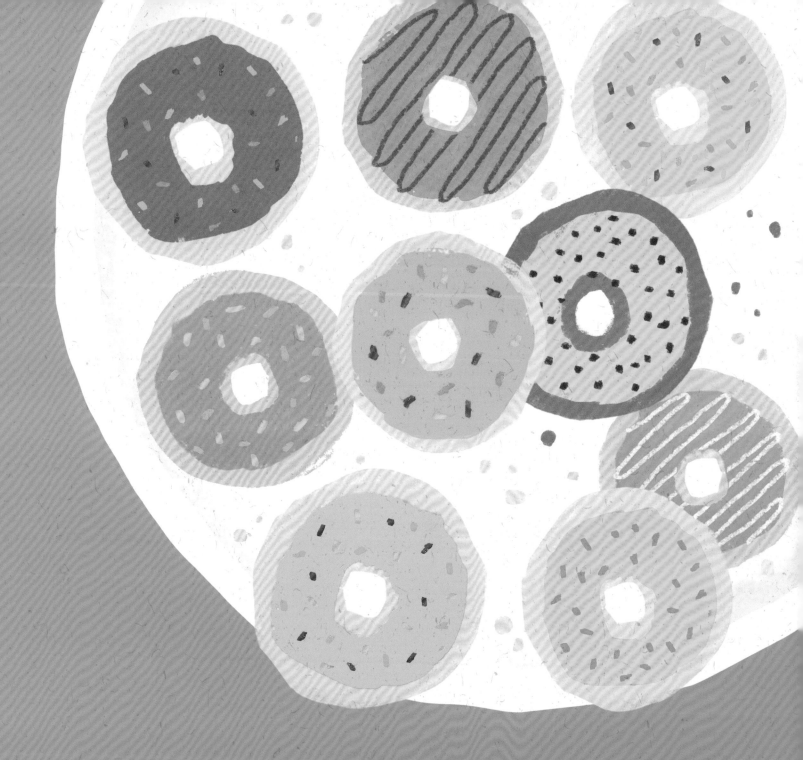

Don't upset Mikey! Turn the page
without touching the donuts.

Hey!
One of my
donuts is **missing!**

Did you touch my donuts?
Keep your fingers away
from them...

**Do NOT
TOUCH!**

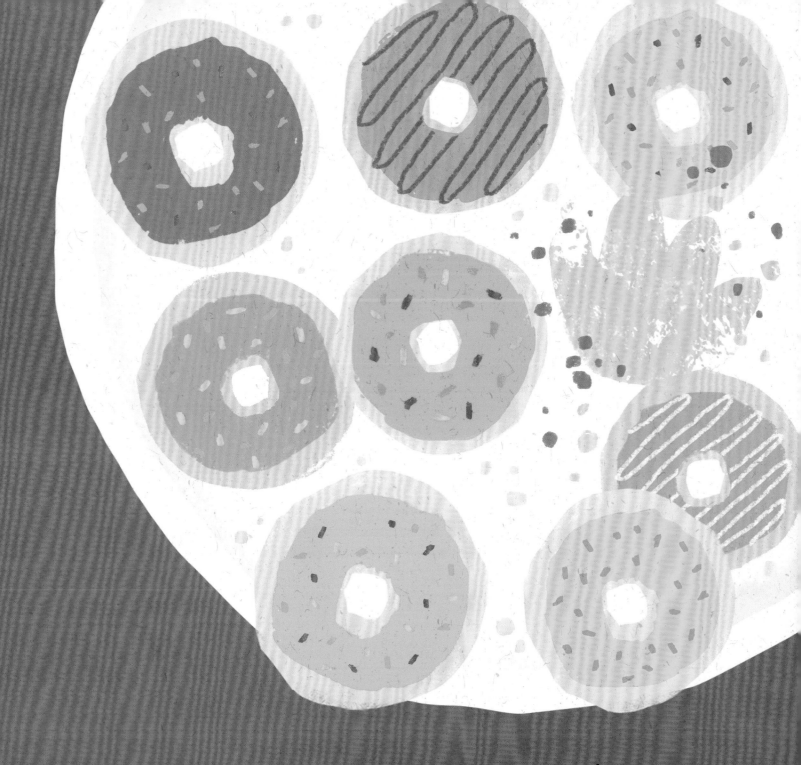

Mikey seems angry! Turn the page without
touching the donuts. Be very careful!

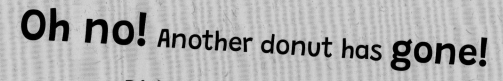

Oh no! Another donut has **gone!**

Did you touch my donuts?
Keep your fingers away from them...

DO
NOT
TOUCH!

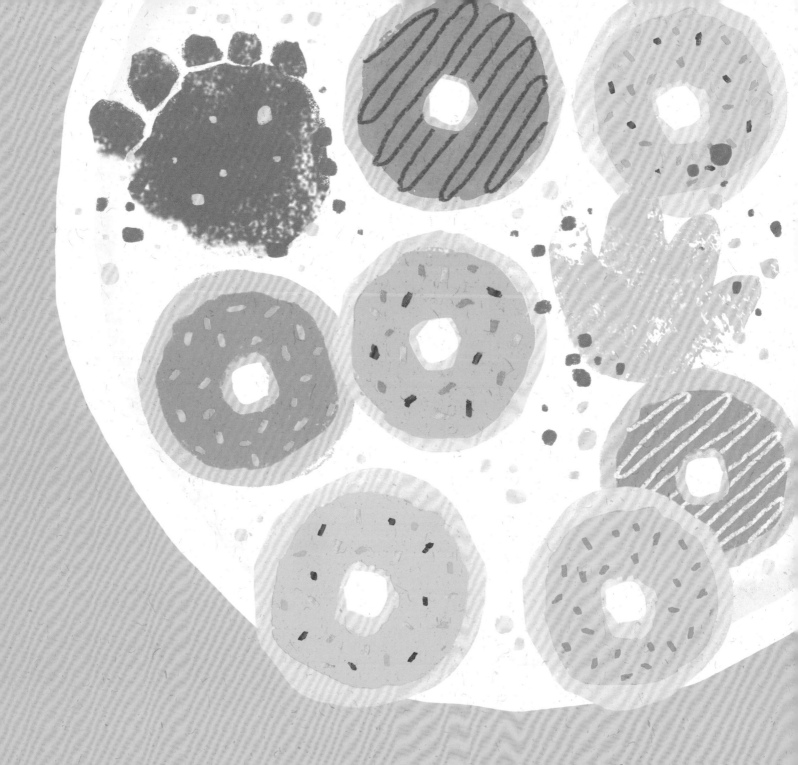

Mikey is really mad now! Turn the page without touching the donuts...not even a crumb!

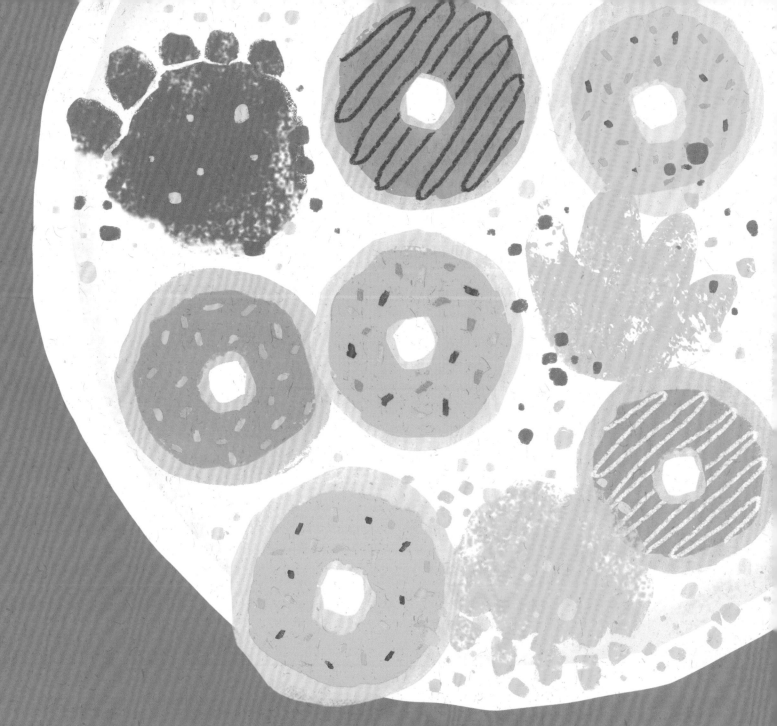

Uh-oh! Mikey thinks **you** have taken his donuts!
Turn the page without touching the donuts.
Mikey is watching you!

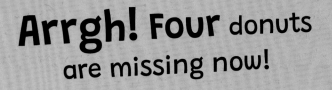

Arrgh! Four donuts are missing now!

Did you touch my donuts? Keep your fingers away from them...

Do NOT TOUCH!

Who is taking Mikey's donuts?
Turn the page without touching the donuts...
or the crumbs...or the frosting!

Roar!
Even **more** donuts have vanished!

Did you touch my donuts?

Keep your fingers away from them...

DO NOT TOUCH!

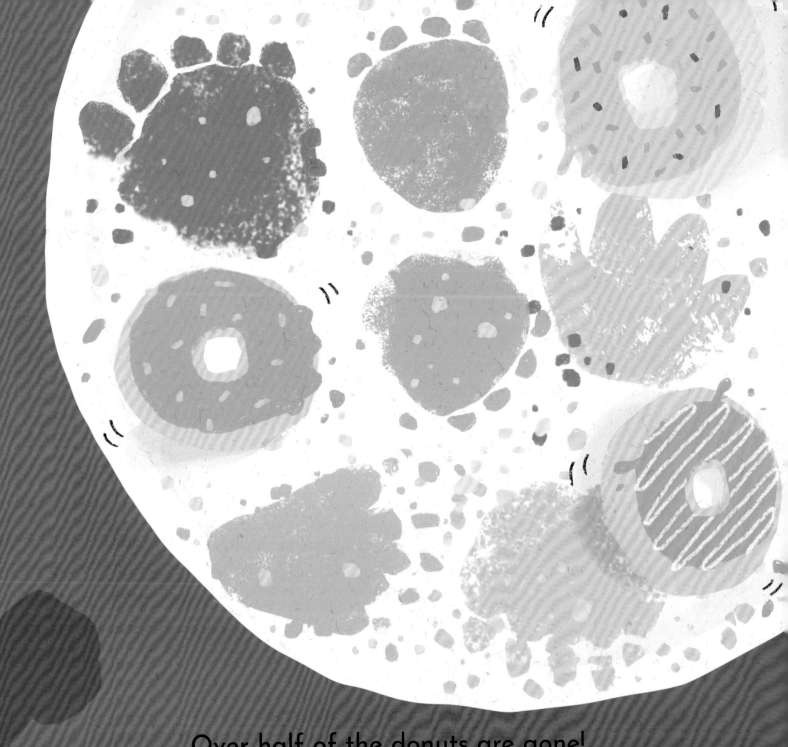

Over half of the donuts are gone!
This means trouble! Turn the page very, VERY, VERY
carefully...without touching the donuts.

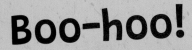
Boo-hoo!
My favorite frosted
donut has **gone!**

Did you touch my donuts?

Keep your
fingers away
from them...

DO
NOT
TOUCH!

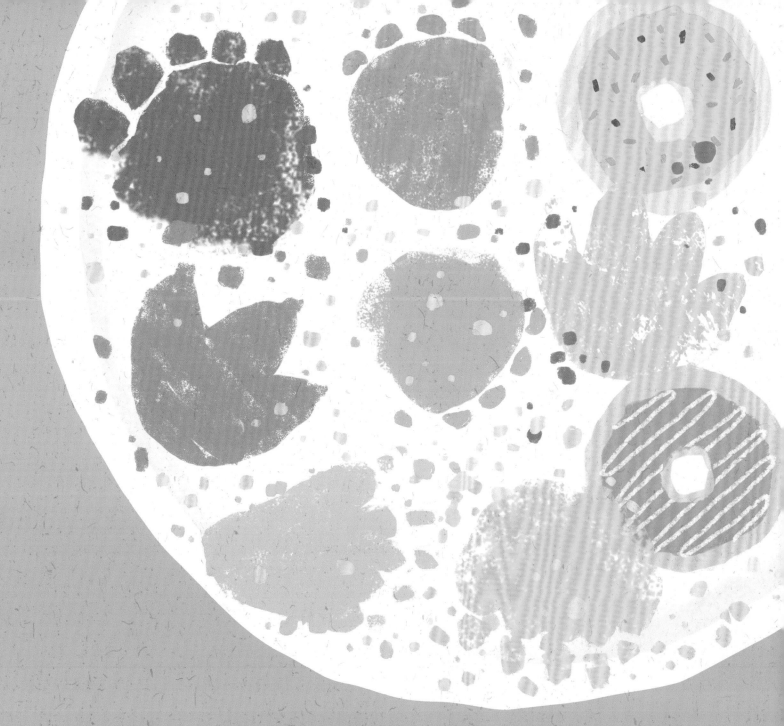

Oh dear! Mikey is really sad!
Turn the page without touching the donuts
and making him more upset.

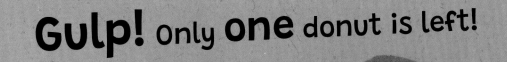

Gulp! only **one** donut is left!

Did you
touch my donuts?
Keep your fingers
away from it...

DO NOT
TOUCH!

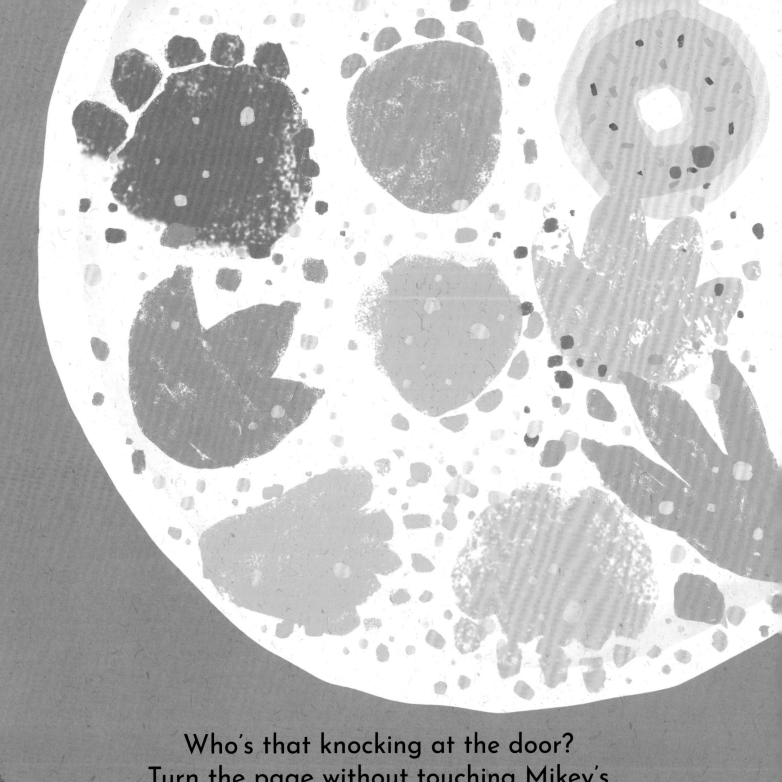

Who's that knocking at the door?
Turn the page without touching Mikey's
very last donut, or the donut-y remains.

Mikey realizes that it is good to share.
But just to be sure, turn the page
without touching that donut!

Sorry!
Would **YOU** like to share my last donut?
Use your fingers...

YOU
CAN
TOUCH!

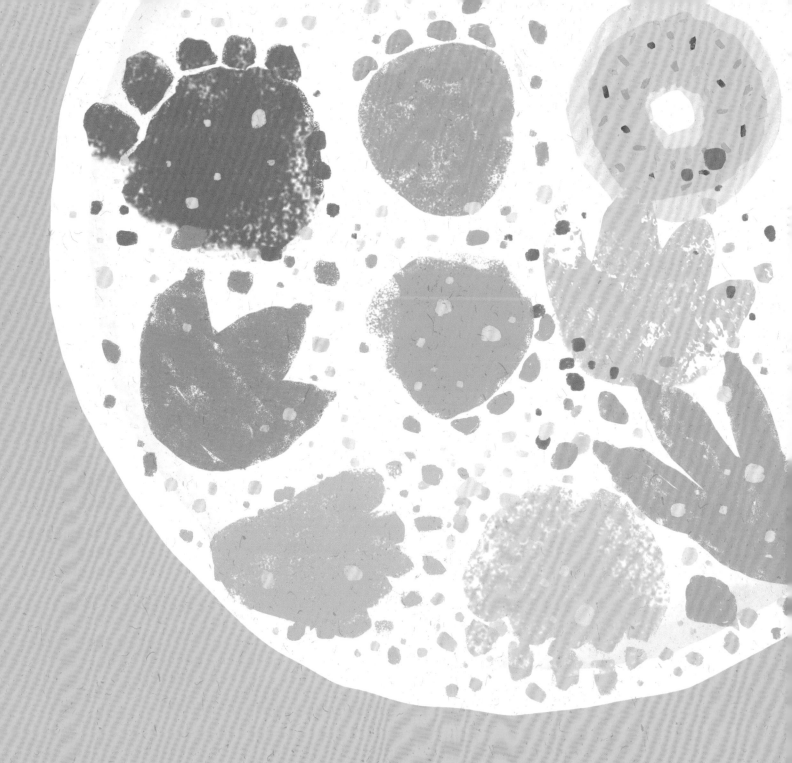

Mikey likes sharing now! Phew!
Turn the page any way you like!

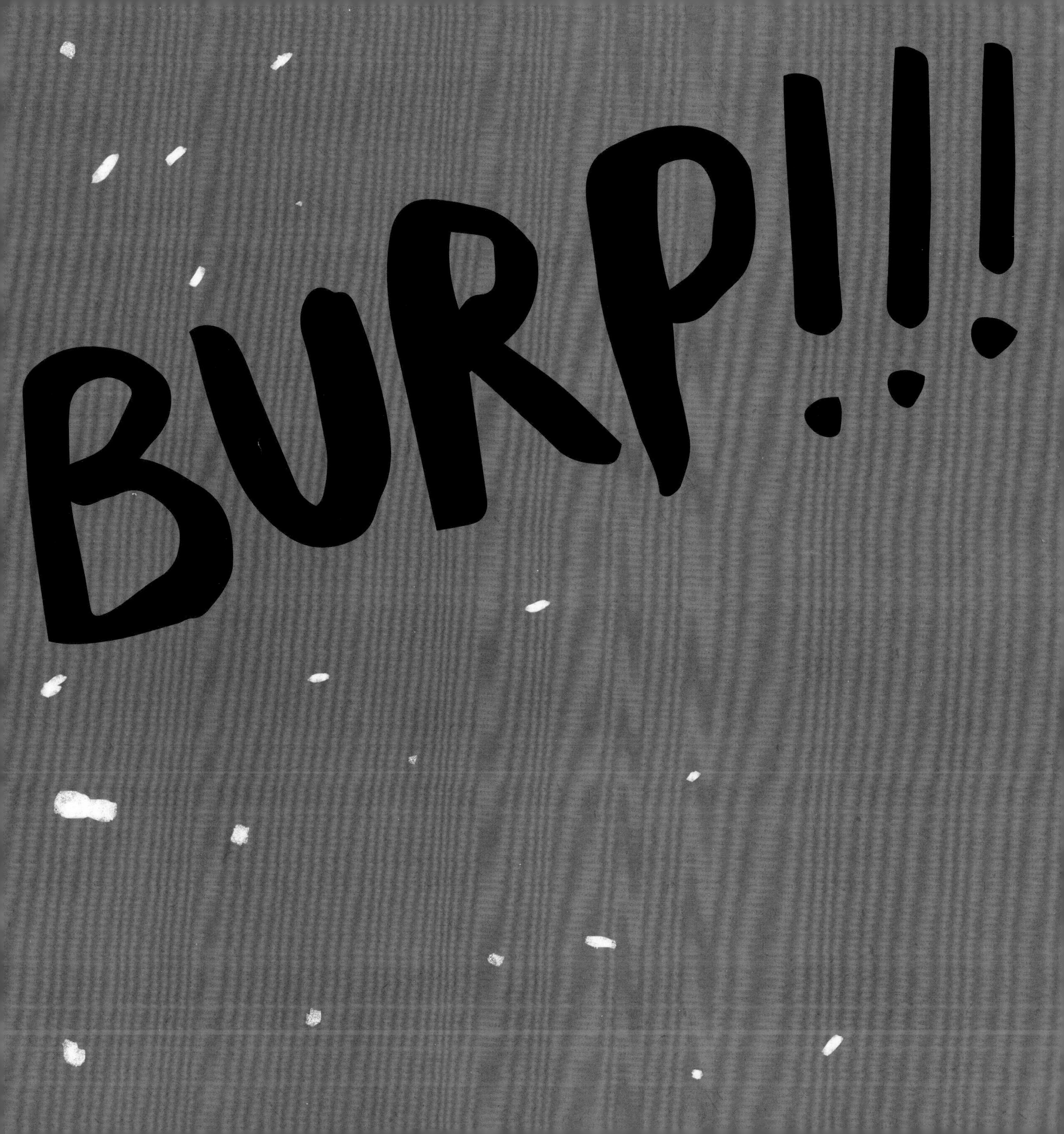
BURP!!!

These donuts are

mine!

Use your fingers to
share them with me!

We're Going on a Dino Hunt!

Written by
Yasmin Bond

Illustrated by
Vicky Lommatzsch

We're going on a dino hunt.
We're going to find a **BIG** one.

What a fun thing to do.
We're <u>not</u> scared!

Oh look...

Dogs!
Yappy, *happy* dogs!

Can't go **over** them.
Can't go **under** them.
Can't go **around** them.
Yikes! Got to go **through** them!

Yap, lick!

Yap, lick!

Yap, lick!

We're going on a dino hunt.
We're going to find a **BIG** one.
What a fun thing to do.
We're <u>not</u> scared!

Oh look...

Cats!
Furry, *purry* cats!

Can't go **over** them.
Can't go **under** them.
Can't go **around** them.
Yikes! Got to go
through them!

Meow, purr!

Meow, purr!

Meow, purr!

We're going on a dino hunt.
We're going to find a **BIG** one.
What a fun thing to do.
We're <u>not</u> scared!

Oh look...

A swamp!
A yucky, *sucky* swamp!

Can't go **over** it.
Can't go **under** it.
Can't go **around** it.
Yikes! Got to go
through it!

Slurp, slop!

Slurp, slop!

Slurp, slop!

We're going on a dino hunt.
We're going to find a **BIG** one.
What a fun thing to do.
We're <u>not</u> scared!

Oh look...

Frogs!
Croaky, *jokey* frogs!

Can't go **over** them.
Can't go **under** them.
Can't go **around** them.
Yikes! Got to go **through** them!

We're going on a dino hunt.
We're going to find a **BIG** one.
What a fun thing to do.
We're <u>not</u> scared!

What's that? A cave! A deep, dark cave.
Can't go **over** it.
Can't go **under** it.
Can't go **around** it.
Yikes! Got to go **through** it!

Bump, *trip!* Bump, *trip!*

Who's there?

Scary, scaly claws!

Big, enormous teeth!

A terrible tail and gigantic feet!

ROAR!!!

It's a DINOSAUR!

Quick, back through the cave.
Bump, trip!
Bump, trip!

Frogs

Skip past the frogs.
Croak, ribbit!
Croak, ribbit!

Run through the yucky swamp.
Slurp, slop!
Slurp, slop!

Swamp

cats

Race by the cats.
Meow, purr!
　　　Meow, purr!

Dash through the dogs.
Yap, lick!
　　Yap, lick!

Dogs

Phew—we're home!

Quick, lock the door and
hide under the bed!

We're <u>not</u> going on a
dino hunt ever again!

The Dinosaur Next Door

Written by

Bobbie Brooks

Illustrated by

Rhys Waters

On the other side of town is the most amazing street.

It's the home of roar-some neighbors that you will love to meet!

FOSSIL STREET

Triceratops lives at number ten,
She's watering her flowers, again.

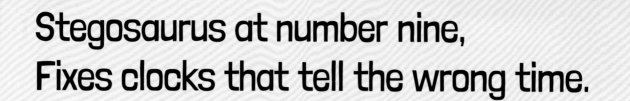

Stegosaurus at number nine,
Fixes clocks that tell the wrong time.

At number eight,
there are two beds,

Spinosaurus thinks it's heaven,
To eat waffles every day at number seven.

Velociraptors practice

flips and tricks,

There's always loud music at number five,
Ankylosaurus loves to dance and jive.

There are lots and lots of roars,
From the T. rex at number four.

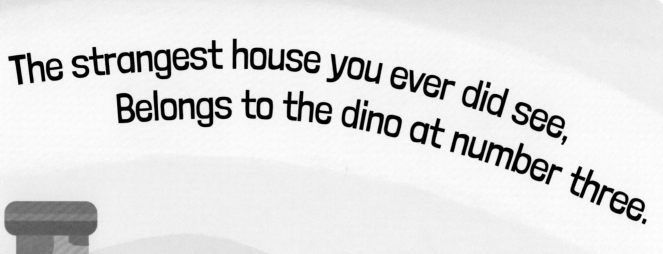

The strangest house you ever did see,
Belongs to the dino at number three.

At number two, who's making a cake?
Allosaurus loves to cook and bake!

So that's the most roar-some street in town,
It's time to go, I hope we see you around!

Valley of the Dinosaurs

Written by
Oakley Graham

Illustrated by
Ben Mantle

Millions of years ago, long before humans existed, Earth belonged to the dinosaurs.

Herds of plant-eating dinosaurs roamed across the land where fierce, meat-eating predators hunted, and pterosaurs ruled the skies.

There wasn't any grass when dinosaurs roamed Earth. Instead, the land was covered in a blanket of conifers and ferns.

At the end of the dinosaurs' time on Earth, early flowers and trees such as oak, beech, walnut, and maple started to appear.

Can you spot the prehistoric creatures who are hiding around the plants and trees?

It's time to meet the dinosaurs
who live in the valley...

There is no mistaking plant-eating Triceratops with three huge horns sticking out of its head and a colorful bony frill around its neck!

Triceratops lived in large herds and used their bony neck frills and horns to defend themselves against predators like Tyrannosaurus rex.

Slow-moving Stegosaurus had large bony plates running along its back and a spiked tail, which it used to defend itself.

Despite being nearly 30 feet long, plant-eating Stegosaurus had a very small brain, which was around the size of a kiwi fruit!

Weighing around 9 tons and at 40 feet long, Tyrannosaurus rex was one of the most deadly dinosaur predators of all time!

Tyrannosaurus rex had a large head
with powerful jaws and dagger-like teeth.
It could run very fast over short distances.

Brachiosaurus had an enormous neck that helped it to eat the fresh fruit and leaves growing high off the ground.

This slow-moving dinosaur giant needed to feed from morning until night simply to stay alive. It grew up to 85 feet in length and weighed around 39 tons!

Pteranodons ruled the skies at the time of the dinosaurs and used their 6-feet-long wings to fly far out to sea to hunt for fish.

Pteranodons' wings were so large in comparison to their feet that they probably had to launch off cliffs to take off.

Before they became extinct
(died out), there were hundreds
of different types of dinosaur.
Do you recognize any of the dinosaurs
who are roaming through the land?

Millions of years later, dinosaurs still
fascinate and amaze humans. They are
totally roar-some!